Red is Best

25 Anniversary Edition

Red is Best

Story · Kathy Stinson

Art · Robin Baird Lewis

Annick Press Ltd.

Toronto + New York + Vancouver

Seventh printing, October 2012

We acknowledge the support of the Canada Council for the Arts, the Ontario Arts Council, and the Government of Canada through the Canada Book Fund (CBF) for our publishing activities.

ONTARIO ARTS COUNCIL
CONSEIL DES ARTS DE L'ONTARIO

Cataloging in Publication

Stinson, Kathy
    Red is best / story, Kathy Stinson ; art, Robin Baird Lewis. – 25th anniversary ed.

First published: 1982.
ISBN-13: 978-1-55451-052-8 (bound)
ISBN-10: 1-55451-052-X (bound)
ISBN-13: 978-1-55451-051-1 (pbk.)
ISBN-10: 1-55451-051-1 (pbk.)

    I. Lewis, Robin Baird II. Title.

PS8587.T56R4 2006   jC813'.54   C2006-901114-1

The text was typeset in Vag Rounded.

Distributed in Canada by: Published in the U.S.A. by:
Firefly Books Ltd.   Annick Press (U.S.) Ltd.
66 Leek Crescent   Distributed in the U.S.A. by:
Richmond Hill, ON   Firefly Books (U.S.) Inc.
L4B 1H1   P.O. Box 1338
                                  Ellicott Station
                                  Buffalo, NY 14205
Printed in China.

Visit us at: www.annickpress.com

Twenty-five years ago, I tried to convince my three-year-old daughter to wear white or blue stockings to nicely match the dress she was wearing. For reasons I couldn't fathom, she insisted on wearing her red ones. Who would have thought our argument would be heard throughout the world? After all, hadn't countless mothers and toddlers waged similar battles before us?

Yet *Red is Best* would soon be found in homes, classrooms, and libraries all over North America. The stubborn little heroine with my daughter's name would become – for readers all over the world – Sally, Sophie, Nanu, Anna, Sanne, Sanoo, Isabella, and simply *kind* (the Dutch word for "child"). Why did this happen?

Is it because so many people like red? Because the book works well in units of study on color? Because its text is simple enough for those learning to read? Or is it because we have all felt misunderstood at times and admire our heroine's ability to assert herself so effectively? I expect it's a combination of these reasons. And of course one more. It's because *rött är bäst. Le rouge, c'est bien mieux. El rojo es el mejor. Rot am schönsten ist. Hoe rooier hoe mooier. Rødt er bedst. Akaga ichiban.* Yes, red is best!
—*Kathy Stinson*

It was a "But of course!" moment for me. That icy January day I bundled up deliberately in a bulky red sweater and my red thermals under my jeans to cope with the frigid drive to my first interview with the publishers of my new illustrating job. Even my earrings were bright red.

My inspiration for the child was no coincidence either. Floating into my mind came that quintessential female child, 3 years old going on 30, who strides through her world with devastating clarity and confident insight. With not a little pity in her kindness, and full of generous enthusiasm, she is more than happy to explain it all, so that you can understand what to her is the obvious.

With a universal appeal to a toddler's view of the world, I designed the art with a classic approach. In the years that followed I witnessed students beaming with delight as they demonstrated a thorough understanding of *Red is Best*, sometimes heightened by the joy that this was their first English-language book. Now our young lady's mantra is heard around the world, translated into many languages and redesigned at least once (to accommodate snowless Venezuela). Long may her robust declaration ring!
—*Robin Baird Lewis*

My mom doesn't
understand about red.

I like my red stockings the best.

My mom says, "Wear these.
Your white stockings look good
with that dress."

But I can jump
higher in my red
stockings.

I like my red stockings the best.

I like my red jacket the best.

My mom says, "You need to wear your blue jacket. It's too cold out for your red jacket."

But how can I be Red Riding
Hood in my blue jacket?

I like my red jacket the best.

I like my red
boots the best.

My mom says, "You
can't wear your red
boots in the snow.
They're just for
rainy weather."

But my red boots
take bigger steps.

I like my red boots the best.

I like my red mitts the best.

My mom says,
"Your brown mitts
are warmer. Your
red mitts have
holes in them."

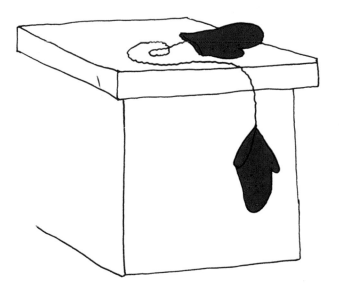

But my red mitts make better snowballs.

I like my red mitts the best.

I like my red pajamas the best.

My mom says, "Your yellow
pajamas will keep you warm
when you kick off your blankets."

But my red pajamas keep the monsters away when I'm sleeping. I like my red pajamas the best.

I like the red cup the best.

My mom says, "Oh Kelly, what difference does it make? I already poured your juice in the green cup."

But juice tastes better in the red cup.

I like the red cup best.

I like my red barrettes the best.

My mom says, "You wear pink
barrettes with a pink dress."

But my red barrettes make my hair laugh.

I like my red barrettes the best.

I like red paint the best.

My mom says, "But Kelly, there is hardly any red paint left. Maybe you could use orange instead."

But red paint puts
singing in my head.

I like the red paint best.

I like red, because
red is best.

Kathy Stinson

Mother of two when she wrote *Red is Best*, Kathy has since added two step-daughters, a daughter-in-law, two sons-in-law, and five grandchildren to her family. Now the author of more than 25 diverse titles, she lives near Guelph, Ontario, with editor Peter Carver. Kathy may not have understood about red 25 years ago, but she does now.

Robin Baird Lewis

Now with decades of experience living and working in the collective arts – privately, publicly, institutionally, commercially, and entrepreneurially – Robin appreciates even more the gifts and instincts that guided her illustrations and overall design for *Red is Best*. A new era of involvement in community arts, music, theater, dance, and literacy projects keeps Robin's home-studio (always open for business!) busy year-round.